Mama, Will It Snow Tonight?

Mama, Will It Snow Tonight?

Nancy White Carlstrom

Illustrated by Paul Tong

BOYDS MILLS PRESS

HONESDALE, PENNSYLVANIA

For Grace Martin and her grandchildren:
Carina Martin; David, Molly, and Tommy Martin;
Maya and Jonathon Perez;
and Elizabeth and Nathan Nicholson
—N.W.C.

For Donna and Leigh, who add the spark to my illustrations
—P. T.

Text copyright © 2009 by Nancy White Carlstrom
Illustrations copyright © 2009 by Paul Tong
All rights reserved

Boyds Mills Press, Inc.
815 Church Street
Honesdale, Pennsylvania 18431
Printed in China

CIP data is available.

First edition
The text of this book is set in 38-point Adobe Caslon.
The illustrations are done in oils.

10 9 8 7 6 5 4 3 2 1

Mama,
will it snow?

Mama,
will it snow?

Mama,
will it snow tonight?

No.

No.

No snow tonight.

Mama, will it snow?
Mama, will it snow?
Mama, will it snow tonight?

The wind is *brrrr*.
The bushes bare.
The berries picked.

Mama, will it snow?
Mama, will it snow?
Mama, will it snow tonight?

Our fur is thick.

Our brown turns white.

Our jam is made.

Mama, will it snow?
Mama, will it snow?
Mama, will it snow tonight?

Soon.
Soon.
Very soon.

It smells like snow.
It sounds like snow.
It feels like snow.

That night they all looked up
at the hazy-lazy, fuzzy moon.

And all the mothers said,
in their own mother way,
"It will snow tonight."

And sure enough . . .

all those mothers were right.